THIS POOLBEG BOOK BELONGS TO:

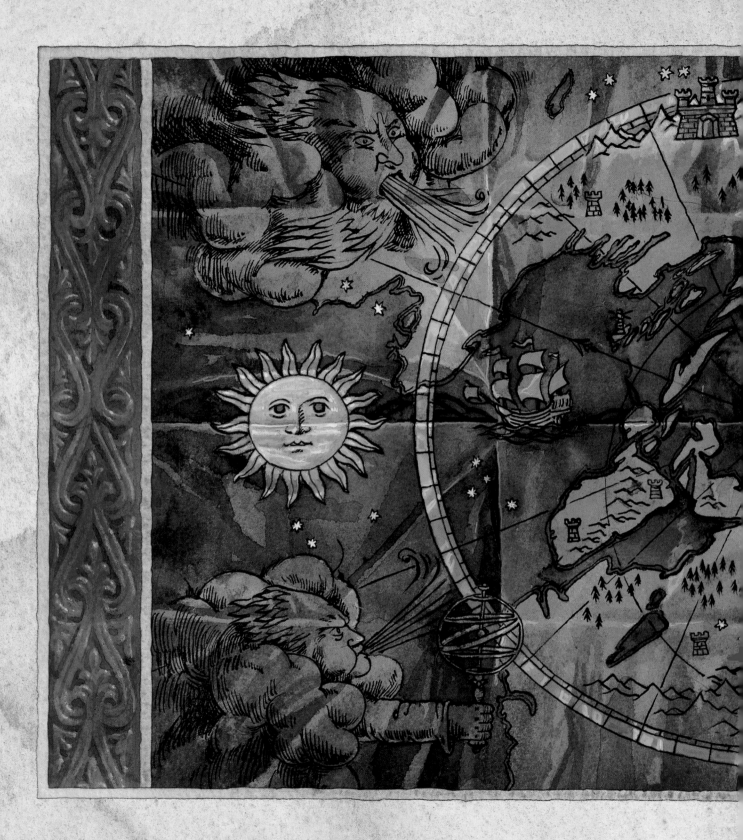

EAST O' THE SUN
AND
WEST O'
THE MOON

Illustrated by
P.J. Lynch

With an
introduction by
Naomi Lewis

Children's
POOLBEG

*For Bill,
Sinéad and
Daniel James*

East o' the Sun and West o' the
Moon is a Norwegian fairy tale
collected by Peter Christen
Asbjørnsen and Jørgen Moe,
and published in their *Norske
Folkeeventyr*, 1844. It was
translated into English by Sir
George Webbe Dasent and
published in his *Popular Tales
from the Norse*, 1859. Only
minor changes have been
made in this book to the
original translation.

This edition published 1996
in conjunction with
Children's Poolbeg
123 Baldoyle Industrial Estate
Baldoyle, Dublin 13

First published 1994 by
Walker Books Ltd, 87 Vauxhall Walk
London SE11 5HJ

2 4 6 8 10 9 7 5 3 1

Introduction © 1991 Naomi Lewis
Illustrations © 1991 P.J. Lynch

Printed in Hong Kong

British Library Cataloguing in Publication Data
A catalogue record for this book is
available from the British Library.

ISBN 1-85371-639-1

Introduction

*From the very start of this marvellous story
you step straight into fairy tale. You will meet a
quest, "far and long", to somewhere not to be
found ("there was no way to that place"), a
spell that must be broken, a bridegroom who
may not be seen in his human form, three
strange hags with golden gifts and a dauntless
girl who takes all magic as it comes, as she
journeys on the impossible road to her wish.
Here are towering crags, forests, trolls and
castles, and a flight through the air on the
North Wind's back to what seems the end of
the world. All these fit together to make a
perfect tale of its kind, a perfect piece of
storytelling.*

*East o' the Sun and West o' the Moon
comes from the great collection of Norwegian
fairy tales (1844) made by Asbjørnsen and
Moe, two young men who had been so much
excited by the work of the Grimm brothers that
they set about gathering the folklore of their
own village people. The first translation into
English was by Sir George Webbe Dasent; his*
Popular Tales from the Norse, *as he called
his book, appeared in 1859, and it is his
version that you are reading here. Dasent was
a quirky, crotchety character, but a great
scholar of folklore, the Northern in particular.*

And he was, as you see, himself a first-rate storyteller, brisk and sparkling, making any reader feel his chosen listener.

It is not surprising that Dasent (like C.S. Lewis) was so captivated by the North. The plots of fairy tales everywhere have many likenesses; what changes them is the place where they are told – the country and the people. Wherever the landscape is wild, the winters long and bitter and the villages small and isolated, magic and mystery thrive. Why should the folk there doubt that trolls live in the forest, as well as wolves and bears; or that animals, who share the same scene and hardships, can speak if they will, and even change into humans and back again?

Readers of fairy tales will have many times met the "animal husband", usually a human prince bewitched. In Lang's Colour Fairy Books you'll find not only Beauty and the Beast and The Frog Prince but an enchanted pig, a hoodie crow, a white wolf, a snake prince and many another. Our "lassie" has more luck than some. The bear was held in the North to be the king of all the animals, respected too by humans for his strength and wisdom. But when the lassie does the forbidden thing and tries with a tallow candle to see the unseen sleeper, she is living out the ancient, classical tale of Cupid and Psyche, which has crossed over many climes and frontiers on its wanderings to the North.

For the bygone village listeners, though, what may well have stirred them most was the episode of the Four Winds, especially the great flight, far and far, on the North Wind's back. To rise into the sky, to cover vast distances at speed – these were almost beyond imagining. The flight can rouse us still. Every story takes with one hand and gives with another. Did Andersen, in neighbouring Denmark, think of this tale as he wrote himself of the winds? Did George MacDonald recall that flight when he set down the greatest of all such stories, old or new, At the Back of the North Wind?

The place that lies at once both east of the sun and west of the moon is still on no ordinary map – though it may have other names. If you are determined, "thither you'll come, late or never," as the old hag says. Since there are no signposts you can start wherever you will. It is the place where the problem is solved, but not too easily; where the wish is granted, if it is truly wished – but not too easily either, for then there would be no story. And if you need to find it again, it will be there, though the journey may be different. What did the lovers do when they had gained the castle? Why, they flitted away together, and as that's both an ending and a beginning, you couldn't devise a better close to the tale.

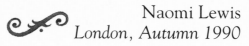 Naomi Lewis
London, Autumn 1990

*O*nce on a time there was a poor husbandman who had so many children that he hadn't much of either food or clothing to give them. Pretty children they all were, but the prettiest was the youngest daughter, who was so lovely there was no end to her loveliness.

Well, one day, 'twas on a Thursday evening late at the fall of the year, the weather was so wild and rough outside that the walls of the cottage shook again. It was cruelly dark, and rain fell and wind blew. There they all sat round the fire busy with this thing and that when, all at once, something gave three taps on the window-pane. Then the father went out to see what was the matter; and, when he got out of doors, what should he see but a big White Bear.

"Good evening to you," said the White Bear.

"The same to you," said the man.

"Will you give me your youngest daughter? If you will, I'll make you as rich as you are now poor," said the Bear.

Well, the man would not be at all sorry to be so rich; but still he thought he must have a bit of a talk with his daughter first; so he went in and told them how there was a great White Bear waiting outside, who had given his word to make them so rich if he could only have the youngest daughter.

The lassie said "No!" outright. Nothing could get her to say anything else; so the man went out and settled it with the White Bear that he should come again the next Thursday evening and get an answer. Meantime he talked his daughter over, and kept on telling her of all the riches they would get, and how well off she would be herself; and so at last she thought better of it, and washed and mended her rags, made herself as smart as she could, and was ready to start. I can't say her packing gave her much trouble.

Next Thursday evening came the White Bear to fetch her, and she got upon his back with her bundle, and off they went. When they had gone a bit of the way, the White Bear said:

"Are you afraid?"

No! she wasn't.

"Well, mind and hold tight by my shaggy coat, and then there's nothing to fear," said the Bear.

So she rode a long, long way, till they came to a great steep hill. There, on the face of it, the White Bear gave a knock, and a door opened, and they came into a castle, where there were many rooms all lit up; rooms gleaming with silver and gold. And there, too, was a table ready laid, and it was all as grand as grand could be.

Then the White Bear gave her a silver bell; and when she wanted anything, she was only to ring it, and she would get it at once.

Well, after she had eaten and drunk, and evening wore on, she got sleepy after her journey, and thought she would like to go to bed, so she rang the bell; and she had scarce taken hold of it before she found herself in a chamber, where there was a bed made, as fair and white as anyone would wish to sleep in, with silken pillows, and curtains fringed with gold. All that was in the room was gold or silver. But when she had gone to bed and put out the light, a man came and laid himself alongside her. That was the White Bear, who threw off his beast shape at night; but she never saw him as a man, for he always came after she had put out the light, and before the day dawned he was up and off again.

So things went on happily for a while; but at last she began to get silent and sorrowful, for she longed to go home to see her father and mother, and brothers and sisters. So one day, when the White Bear asked what it was that she lacked, she said it was so dull and lonely there, and how she longed to go home to see her father and mother, and brothers and sisters, and that was why she was so sad and sorrowful, because she couldn't get to them.

"Well, well!" said the Bear, "perhaps there's a cure for all this; but you must promise me one thing, not to talk alone with your mother, but only when the rest are by to hear; for she'll take you by the hand and try to lead you into a room alone to talk; but you must mind and not do that, else you'll bring bad luck on both of us."

So one Sunday, the White Bear came and said now they could set off to see her father and mother. Well, off they started, she sitting on his back; and they went far and long. At last they came to a grand house, and there her brothers and sisters were running about out of doors at play, and everything was so pretty, 'twas a joy to see.

"This is where your father and mother live now," said the White Bear; "but don't forget what I told you, else you'll make us both unlucky."

No! bless her, she'd not forget; and when she had reached the house, the White Bear turned right about and left her.

Then she went in to see her father and mother, and there was such joy, there was no end to it. None of them thought they could thank her enough for all she had done for them. Now they had everything they wished, as good as good could be, and they all wanted to know how she got on where she lived.

Well, she said it was very good to live where she did; she had all she wished. What she said besides I don't know, but I don't think any of them had the right end of the stick, or that they got much out of her.

So, in the afternoon, after they had done dinner, all happened as the White Bear had said. Her mother wanted to talk with her alone in her bedroom; but she minded what the White Bear had said, and wouldn't go upstairs. "Oh, what we have to talk about will keep," she said, and put her mother off.

But somehow or other, her mother got round her at last, and she had to tell her the whole story. So she said how every night, when she had gone to bed, a man came and lay down beside her as soon as she had put out the light; and how she never saw him, because he was always up and away before the morning dawned; and how she went about woeful and sorrowing, for she thought she should so like to see him; and how all day long she walked about there alone, and how dull and dreary and lonesome it was.

"My!" said her mother, "it may well be a Troll you slept with! But now I'll teach you a lesson how to set eyes on him. I'll give you a bit of candle, which you can carry home in your bosom. Just light that while he is asleep, but take care not to drop the tallow on him."

Yes! she took the candle, and hid it in her bosom, and as night drew on, the White Bear came and fetched her away.

When they had gone a bit of the way, the White Bear asked if all hadn't happened as he had said.

Well, she couldn't say it hadn't.

"Now, mind," said he, "if you have listened to your mother's advice, you have brought bad luck on us both, and then all that has passed between us will be as nothing."

No, she said, she hadn't listened to her mother's advice.

So when she reached home, and had gone to bed, it was the old story over again. There came a man who lay down beside her. But at dead of night, when she heard he slept, she got up and struck a light, lit the candle, and let the light shine on him. And so she saw that he was the loveliest Prince one ever set eyes on, and she fell so deep in love with him on the spot, that she thought she couldn't live if she didn't give him a kiss there and then. And so she did. But as she kissed him, she dropped three hot drops of tallow on his shirt, and he woke up.

"What have you done?" he cried. "Now you have made us both unlucky, for had you held out only this one year, I had been freed. For I have a stepmother who has bewitched me, so that I am a White Bear by day, and a Man by night. But now all ties are snapt between us; now I must set off from you to her. She lives in a castle which stands east o' the sun and west o' the moon, and there, too, is a Princess with a nose three ells long, and she's the wife I must have now."

She wept and took it ill, but there was no help for it – go he must.

Then she asked if she mightn't go with him.

No, she mightn't.

"Tell me the way then," she said, "and I'll search you out; *that* surely I may get leave to do."

Yes, she might do that, he said, but there was no way to the place. It lay east o' the sun and west o' the moon, and thither she'd never find her way.

The next morning, when she woke up, both Prince and castle were gone, and there she lay on a little green patch, in the midst of a gloomy thick wood, and by her side lay the same bundle of rags she had brought with her from her old home.

So when she had rubbed the sleep out of her eyes, and wept till she was tired, she set out on her way, and walked many, many days, till she came to a lofty crag. Under it sat an old hag who was playing with a gold apple, which she tossed about. The lassie asked her if she knew the way to the Prince who lived with his stepmother in the castle that lay east o' the sun and west o' the moon, and who was to marry the Princess with a nose three ells long.

"How did you come to know about him?" asked the old hag. "Or maybe you are the lassie who ought to have had him?"

Yes, she was.

"So, so; it's you, is it?" said the old hag. "Well, all I know about him is that he lives in the castle that lies east o' the sun and west o' the moon, and thither you'll come, late or never; but still you may have the loan of my horse, and on him you can ride to my next neighbour. Maybe she'll be able to tell you; and when you get there, just give the horse a switch under the left ear and beg him to be off home. And, stay! this gold apple you may take with you."

She got upon the horse, and rode a long long time, till she came to another crag, under which sat another old hag, with a gold carding-comb.

The lassie asked her if she knew the way to the castle that lay east o' the sun and west o' the moon, and she answered, like the first old hag, that she knew nothing about it, except that it was east o' the sun and west o' the moon.

"And thither you'll come, late or never. But you shall have the loan of my horse to my next neighbour – maybe she'll tell you all about it; and when you get there, just switch the horse under the left ear and beg him to be off home."

And this old hag gave her the golden carding-comb – it might be she'd find some use for it, she said. So the lassie got up on the horse, and rode a far far way and a weary time; and at last she came to another great crag, under which sat another old hag, spinning with a gold spinning-wheel.

She asked her, too, if she knew the way to the Prince, and where the castle was that lay east o' the sun and west o' the moon.

So it was the same thing over again.

"Maybe it's you who ought to have had the Prince?" said the old hag.

Yes, it was.

But she didn't know the way a bit better than the other two. East o' the sun and west o' the moon it was, she knew – that was all.

"And thither you'll come, late or never. But I'll lend you my horse, and then I think you'd best ride to the East Wind and ask him; maybe he knows those parts, and can blow you thither. But when you get to him, you need only give the horse a switch under the left ear, and he'll trot home of himself."

And so, too, she gave her the gold spinning-wheel. "Maybe you'll find a use for it," said the old hag.

Then on she rode many many days, a weary time, before she got to the East Wind's house. But at last she did reach it, and then she asked the East Wind if he could tell her the way to the Prince who dwelt east o' the sun and west o' the moon. Yes, the East Wind had often heard tell of it, the Prince and the castle, but he couldn't tell the way, for he had never blown so far.

"But, if you wish, I'll go with you to my brother the West Wind – maybe he knows, for he's much stronger. If you will just get on my back I'll carry you thither."

Yes, she got on his back, and I should just think they went briskly along.

When they got there, they went into the West Wind's house, and the East Wind said the lassie he had brought was the one who ought to have had the Prince who lived in the castle east o' the

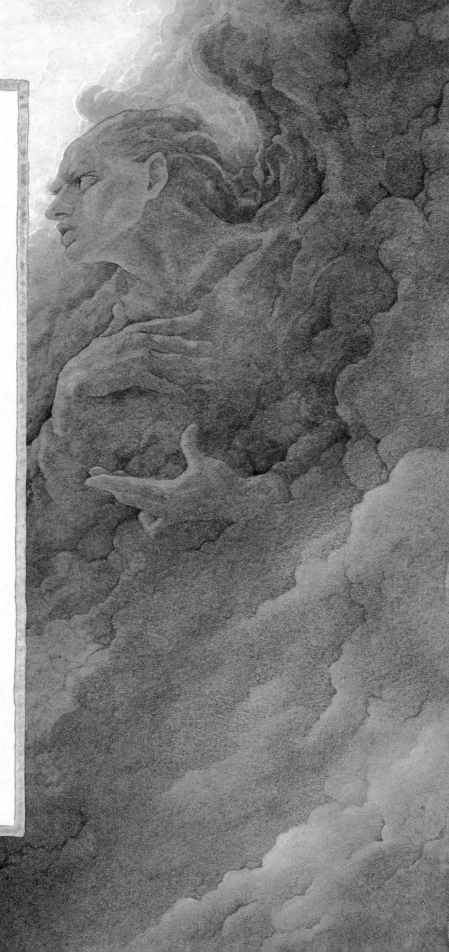

sun and west o' the moon; and so she had set out to seek him, and he had come with her, and would be glad to know if the West Wind knew how to get to the castle.

"Nay," said the West Wind, "that far I've never blown. But if you will, I'll go with you to our brother the South Wind, for he's much stronger than either of us, and he has flapped his wings far and wide. Maybe he'll tell you. You can get on my back, and I'll carry you to him."

Yes! she got on his back, and so they travelled to the South Wind, and weren't so very long on the way either, I should think.

When they got there, the West Wind asked him if he could tell her the way to the castle that lay east o' the sun and west o' the moon, for it was she who ought to have had the Prince who lived there.

"You don't say so! That's her, is it?" said the South Wind.

"Well, I have blustered about in most places in my time, but so far have I never blown. But, if you wish, I'll take you to my brother the North Wind; he is the oldest and strongest of the whole lot of us, and if he doesn't know where it is, you'll never find anyone in the world to tell you. You can get on my back, and I'll carry you thither."

Yes! she got on his back, and away he went from his house at a fine rate. And this time, too, she wasn't long on her way. And when they got to the North Wind's house, he was so wild and cross, cold puffs came from him a long way off.

"BLAST YOU BOTH, WHAT DO YOU WANT?" he roared out, and it struck them with an icy shiver.

"Well," said the South Wind, "you needn't be so foul-mouthed, for here I am, your brother, the South Wind, and

here is the lassie who ought to have had the Prince who dwells in the castle that lies east o' the sun and west o' the moon, and now she wants to ask you if you ever were there, and can tell her the way, for she would be so glad to find him again."

"YES, I KNOW WELL ENOUGH WHERE IT IS," said the North Wind. "Once in my life I blew an aspen leaf thither, but I was so tired I couldn't blow a puff for ever so many days after. But if you really wish to go, and aren't afraid to come along with me, I'll take you on my back and see if I can blow you there."

Yes! with all her heart; she must and would get there if it were possible in any way; and as for fear, however madly he went, she wouldn't be at all afraid.

"Very well then," said the North Wind, "but you must sleep here tonight, for we must have the whole day before us, if we're to get there at all."

Early next morning, the North Wind woke her, and puffed himself up, and blew himself out, and made himself so stout and big, 'twas gruesome to look at him; and so off they went – high up through the air, as if they would never stop till they got to the world's end.

Down here below, there was such a storm it threw down long tracts of wood and many houses, and when it swept over the great sea, ships foundered by hundreds.

So they tore on and on – no one can believe how far they went – and still they went over the sea, and the North Wind got more and more weary, and so out of breath he could scarce bring out a puff, and his wings drooped and drooped till, at last, he sunk so low that the crests of the waves dashed over his heels.

"Are you afraid?" said the North Wind.

No! she wasn't.

But they weren't very far from land; and the North Wind had still enough strength left in him that he managed to throw her up on the shore under the windows of the castle which lay east o' the sun and west o' the moon; but then he was so weak and worn out, he had to stay there and rest many days before he could get home again.

ext morning, the lassie sat down under the castle window and began to play with the gold apple, and the first person she saw was the Long-nose who was to have the Prince.

"What do you want for your gold apple, you lassie?" said the Long-nose, and threw up the window.

"It's not for sale, for gold or money," said the lassie.

"If it's not for sale for gold or money, what is it that you will sell it for? You may name your own price," said the Princess.

"Well! if I may get to the Prince who lives here, and be with him tonight, you shall have it," said the lassie whom the North Wind had brought.

Yes! she might; that could be done. So the Princess got the gold apple. But when the lassie came up to the Prince's bedroom at night, he was fast asleep; she called him and shook him, and between whiles she wept sore, but for all she could do, she couldn't wake him up. Next morning, as soon as day broke, the Princess with the long nose came and drove her out again.

So, in the daytime, she sat down under the castle window and began to card with her golden carding-comb, and the same thing happened. The Princess asked what she wanted for it; and she said it wasn't for sale for gold or money, but if she might get leave to go up to the Prince and be with him that night, the Princess should have it.

But when she went up she found him fast asleep again, and for all she called, and shook, and wept, and prayed, she couldn't get life into him; and as soon as the first grey peep of day came, then the Princess with the long nose came and chased her out again.

So, in the daytime, the lassie sat down under the castle window, and began to spin with her golden spinning-wheel; and that, too, the Princess with the long nose wanted to have. So she threw up the window and asked what she wanted for it. The lassie said, as she had said twice before, it wasn't for sale for gold or money, but if she might go up to the Prince who was there, and be with him alone that night, she might have it.

Yes! she might do that and welcome.

But now, you must know there were some poor folk who had been carried off there, and as they sat in their room which was next to the Prince's, they had heard how a woman had been in there, and wept and prayed and called to him two nights running, and they told the Prince.

That evening, when the Princess came with her sleepy drink, the Prince made as if he drank, but threw it over his shoulder, for he could guess it was a sleepy drink. So, when the lassie came in, she found the Prince wide awake; and then she told him the whole story of how she had come there.

"Ah," said the Prince, "you've just come in the very nick of time, for tomorrow is to be our wedding-day; but now I won't have the Long-nose, and you are the only woman in the world who can set me free. I'll beg the Long-nose to wash the shirt which has the three spots of tallow on it; she'll say yes, but that's a work no Troll can do, and so I'll say that I won't have any other for my bride than the woman who can wash them out, and ask you to do it."

So there was great joy and love between them all that night.

The next day, when the wedding was to be, the Prince said, "First of all, I'd like to see what my bride is fit for."

"Yes!" said the stepmother, with all her heart.

"Well," said the Prince, "I've got a fine shirt which I'd like for my wedding shirt, but somehow or other it has got three spots of tallow on it, which I must have washed out; and I have sworn never to take any other bride than the woman who's able to do that. If she can't, she's not worth having."

Well, that was no great thing, they said, so they agreed, and she with the

long nose began to wash away as hard as she could, but the more she rubbed and scrubbed, the bigger the spots grew.

"Ah!" said the old hag, her mother, "you can't wash; let me try."

But she hadn't long taken the shirt in hand, before it got far worse than ever, and with all her rubbing and wringing and scrubbing, the spots grew bigger and blacker, and the darker and uglier was the shirt.

Then all the other Trolls began to wash, but the longer it lasted, the blacker and uglier the shirt grew, till at last it was as black all over as if it had been up the chimney.

"Ah!" said the Prince. "You're none of you worth a straw: you can't wash. Why, there outside sits a beggar lassie and I'll be bound she knows how to wash better than the whole lot of you. COME IN, LASSIE!" he shouted.

Well, in she came.

"Can you wash this shirt clean, lassie, you?" said he.

"I don't know," said she, "but I think I can."

And almost before she had taken it and dipped it in the water, it was as white as driven snow, and whiter still.

"Yes! you are the lassie for me," said the Prince.

At that, the old hag flew into such a rage she burst on the spot, and the Princess with the long nose after her, and the whole pack of Trolls after her – at least I've never heard a word about them since.

As for the Prince and Princess, they set free all the poor folk who had been carried off and shut up there; and they took with them all the silver and gold, and flitted away as far as they could from the castle that lay

EAST O' THE SUN AND WEST O' THE MOON.

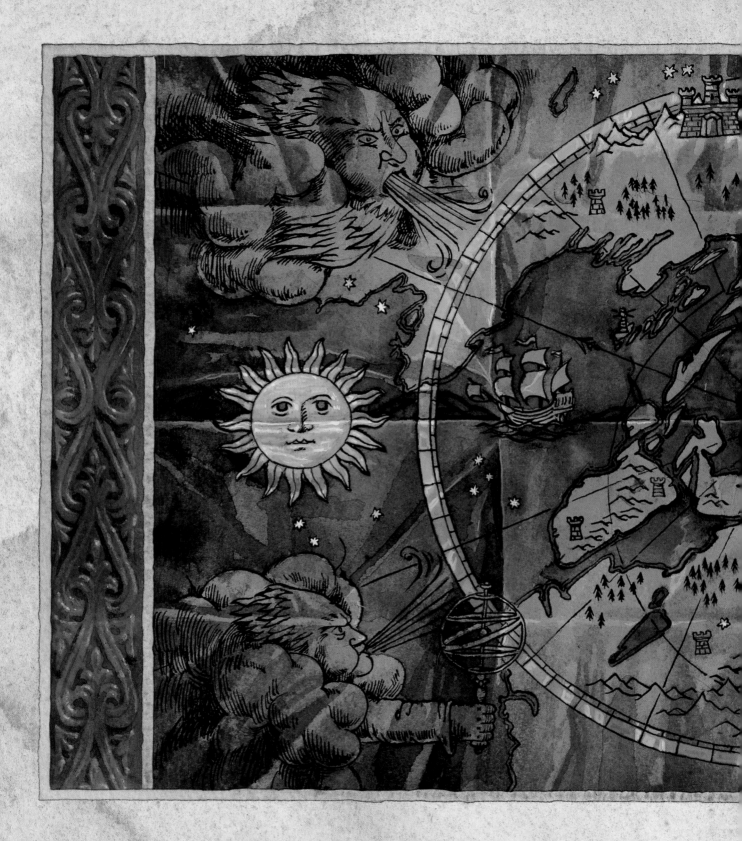

MORE POOLBEG PICTURE BOOKS
For You to Enjoy

THE KING OF IRELAND'S SON
by Brendan Behan / P.J. Lynch

When the King of Ireland sends his three sons to discover the source of heavenly music that can be heard throughout his kingdom, the youngest prince finds a beautiful maiden held captive by a fierce giant . . .

1-85371-622-7   £9.99

CATKIN
by Antonia Barber / P.J. Lynch

When a small girl is taken away by the Little People, it is her tiny cat who goes after her to secure her release . . .

"As an original fairy tale it could not be bettered; a rounded, resonant text together with masterly illustrations by P.J. Lynch." *The Bookseller*

1-85371-468-2   £9.99

THE CHRISTMAS MIRACLE OF JONATHAN TOOMEY
by Susan Wojciechowski / P.J. Lynch

The moving and memorable tale of a sad heart's nativity . . .

"Poignantly illustrated with the contemplative, emotional paintings of P.J. Lynch, Ireland's treasure." *Children's Book Review Magazine*

1-85371-535-2   £9.99

THE SNOW QUEEN
by Hans Christian Andersen / P.J. Lynch

The classic fairy tale of the Snow Queen's abduction of Kay to her frozen palace, and his subsequent heroic rescue by Gerda, his brave friend, retold in this new edition with rich and magical illustrations by P.J. Lynch.

"Stunning illustrations . . . dramatic rich colouring combines with ethereal white, grey and silver to provide haunting interpretation." *Children's Books in Ireland*

1-85371-669-3   £9.99

THE QUEEN OF ARAN'S DAUGHTER
by Maura Laverty / Barry Castle

An original collection of fairy stories set in the west of Ireland.

"Each tale is a gem of storytelling told in rich, musical words." *The Sunday Tribune*

1-85371-448-8   £12.99

TOPSY-TURVY TALES
by Sarah Cunningham

Four famous fairy tale heroines swap places with hilarious results!

"*Topsy-Turvy Tales* is a delight, its brightly coloured affectionately funny graphics perfectly in tune with the subversive twist in the story." *The Tribune Magazine*

1-85371-428-3   £3.99

POOLBEG